Stornoway Primary School
Jamieson Drive
Stornoway
Isle of Lewis
HS1 2LF
Tel: 01851 703418/703621
Fax: 01851 706257
E Mail: stornoway-primary@cne-siar.gov.uk

D1421615

For everyone at Brindle Gregson Lane Primary School

Reprinted 2011
First published 2010 by
A & C Black Publishers Ltd
36 Soho Square, London, W1D 3QY

www.acblack.com
www.damianharvey.co.uk

Text copyright © 2010 Damian Harvey
Illustrations copyright © 2010 Ned Joliffe

The rights of Damian Harvey and Ned Joliffe to be identified as
the author and illustrator of this work have been asserted by them in
accordance with the Copyrights, Designs and Patents Act 1988.

ISBN 978-1-4081-1386-8

A CIP catalogue for this book is available from the British Library.

This book is produced using paper that is made from wood
grown in managed, sustainable forests. It is natural, renewable and
recyclable. The logging and manufacturing processes conform
to the environmental regulations of the country of origin.

Printed and bound in Great Britain
by CPI Cox & Wyman, Reading, RG1 8EX.

THE MUDCRUSTS

MONSTROUS MAMMOTHS

Damian Harvey

Illustrated by Ned Joliffe

A & C Black • London

Chapter ONE

A scrawny, brown rat scurried past Lowbrow Mudcrust's foot and scampered into the cave. Lowbrow hated rats. Usually, he would have tried to catch it. But today he wasn't feeling well. So instead, he watched as the pest grabbed an egg and ran off with it held tightly in its mouth.

"Hey!" cried Flora. "Those eggs are for *our* dinner."

A big hunting spear crashed against the cave wall and went rolling across the floor, just missing the rat.

"Hey!" Flora cried again. "I've *told* you not to throw that in the cave."

"Don't worry," laughed Bogweed. "Fungus won't hit anything. He never does!"

Fungus scowled at his younger brother and picked up the spear.

"Why don't you take him hunting?" said Flora, turning to her husband.

Lowbrow sneezed and shook his head. "We'll go tomorrow," he groaned.

"You said that yesterday," said Flora. "And you've only got a cold. If Bogweed hadn't found these eggs, we'd have nothing to eat. It's a good job he thought of climbing further up the mountain to look for nests."

Fungus glared at his brother. "Ooooh!" he said. "Big brave Bogweed found some eggs. I hope they didn't try to bite."

Bogweed was busy making a long length of rope out of pieces of vine. His face went bright red and he glared back at Fungus. "At least I came back with *something*," he said. "Last time *you* went hunting, you didn't even catch a cold."

"Shut up, Bogstench," snarled Fungus, stomping out of the cave. "I'll catch something for dinner today. *Just* you wait and see."

"Will you go with him, dear?" sighed Flora, looking at Bogweed. "I don't want Fungus going out on his own."

"Me!" cried Bogweed. "What can *I* do? You know I'm no good at hunting."

"But you've got *brains*," said Flora. "Make sure he doesn't do anything silly."

Bogweed reluctantly put down the rope and picked up a spear. Then he set off after his brother. He remembered the last time he'd gone hunting with Fungus. The wild boar they'd been chasing had gone mad, the whole swamp had become flooded and their home had sunk in the mud. It had been a complete disaster. Hopefully things would work out better this time.

Fungus was heading along the path that led to their uncle, Chief Hawknose's

10

cave. From there, it went down towards the edge of the forest and on to Slimepool Swamp. Bogweed was sure his brother wouldn't be going to the swamp, but he knew how much Fungus hated the forest, so he didn't think he'd be heading there, either.

"Where are we going?" he called.

Fungus looked over his shoulder. He scowled when he saw his brother.

"Go away, Stinkweed," he shouted. "*We're* not going anywhere. *I'm* going hunting on my own."

"Mum told me to come, too," said Bogweed. "You *know* it isn't safe to go by yourself."

"Fine!" snapped Fungus. "Just make sure you don't get in my way."

As they passed Chief Hawknose's cave, Bogweed stopped to say hello to their cousin, Mere. Fungus kept on walking.

"Where are you boys off to?" said Chief Hawknose with a grin.

"Dad's not feeling well," explained Bogweed. "So we're out to catch something for dinner."

"What!" cried Chief Hawknose, pretending to look frightened. "Well,

if you two are going hunting, *we'd* better stay inside where it's safe."

Mere rolled her eyes. "Just ignore him," she said. "He's only teasing."

Bogweed smiled weakly. No wonder Dad doesn't like Chief Hawknose, he thought. He can be *really* annoying.

"Don't go too far away," said Fauna, the chief's wife. "There's a storm coming."

Bogweed looked up at the sky as he set off after his brother. Even though winter was almost upon them, it had been a warm day, but now heavy clouds were drifting over the valley. Fauna was right. There *was* a storm coming.

Fungus was already at the bottom of Icecap Mountain, making his way along the path by the edge of the forest. Bogweed hurried to catch up with him.

As they walked, Fungus kept glancing nervously at the trees. There were bears, wolves and all sorts of other creatures living in the forest, and it was a dangerous place to go. After coming face to face with a family of sabre-toothed tigers last week, Fungus had sworn he'd never go back there again.

"Why are we going to the swamp?"

asked Bogweed. "You know there won't be any wild boar there now. It's *much* too wet."

Fungus stopped and turned to glare at his brother. "Of *course* I know that," he said. "That's why we're *not* going to the swamp."

"Well, where *are* we going then?" asked Bogweed. "There's nowhere else at this end of the valley."

"We're going into the forest," snarled Fungus.

Bogweed couldn't believe his ears. "But you're frightened of the forest," he said.

"No, I'm not," snapped Fungus. "I'm not frightened of *anything*. You'll see."

And with that, he marched off through the long grass towards the trees.

Flora had told Bogweed to make sure his brother didn't do anything silly, and going into the forest was definitely something silly. For a moment, he watched in disbelief as Fungus disappeared into the gloomy darkness. Then he ran after him. If Fungus was going into the forest, then he had to follow. But he'd have to be quick if he was going to keep up with his brother.

Chapter Two

Fungus stomped through the undergrowth in a rage. Brambles scratched at his legs and prickled his arms, but he was determined nothing would stop him. He ducked beneath thick branches and pushed thinner ones out of the way.

He was fed up of his weedy little brother getting all the attention. Everyone thought Bogweed was so clever – finding eggs for supper, and making a big wooden mammoth to frighten away the sabre-toothed tiger. Well, he would show them. He wasn't going home today until he'd caught something to eat and proved once and for all that *he* was the better hunter.

Behind, Fungus could hear his brother trying to keep up.

"Wait for me!" called Bogweed.

Fungus ignored him and kept on walking, using his spear to hack his way through a tangle of vines.

In front of him, a large, fat bird shot out of the undergrowth and went squawking and clucking into the bushes, flapping its stubby wings.

Fungus stood still for a moment, his heart pounding. The bird had startled him and he'd *almost* let out a loud squeal. Bogweed would have found that *very* funny. But what was worse, he knew his dad would have *seen* the bird and caught it for their dinner. He'd have to be more alert in future.

Bogweed came clomping through the bushes.

Fungus looked round and pulled a face. "Sssh!" he hissed. "You're frightening the animals. We'll never catch anything if you make all that noise.

Bogweed stood panting for a moment, trying to get his breath back. His face was bright red and he kept looking round nervously, as if he expected something to jump out of the trees at any moment.

For some reason, seeing Bogweed looking worried actually made Fungus feel better. He'd always thought he was the only one that didn't like being in the forest. Stepping over the large bird's nest, he pushed his way through a prickly bush and found himself on what looked like a small path. But it wasn't the sort of path their tribe would have made; this one was narrow and overgrown in places.

Fungus went into a half crouch, like he'd seen their dad do, and crept along with his hunting spear held out in front of him. He had no idea what had made the path – perhaps a wild boar or maybe even a bear. But whatever it was, he wanted to be ready for it.

A little way ahead of them, the path was completely blocked by a huge, fallen

tree. Being careful not to slip on the mossy bark, Fungus clambered on top of the trunk and stood up to get a good look around.

As he stood there, he noticed something very strange. The forest was usually full of sounds. Birds squeaking and chirping. Animals snarling, grunting and howling. But, for once, everything had gone very quiet.

Too quiet.

And that could only mean one thing...

Trouble.

As Fungus listened, the silence of the forest seemed to roar in his ears. Carefully, he crouched down and held his breath as he looked around for predators. He could hear his heart beating in his chest, but nothing else.

Then something touched his shoulder.

Fungus screamed and dropped his spear. His feet slipped on the mossy tree trunk and he almost fell off. Noise erupted from the branches around them as startled birds took to the air. Fungus leapt to his feet and glared at Bogweed, realising it had been his brother who had touched him. "You little weasel," he began. "I should –" Then he stopped.

Bogweed was staring wide-eyed at something behind him.

Very slowly, Fungus turned round and just managed to catch a glimpse of a large shape as it vanished into the forest.

"What was that?" he whispered, hardly daring to move.

Bogweed shook his head. "I'm not sure," he whispered back. "I couldn't see properly, but it looked a bit like –"

"It was a mammoth," interrupted Fungus, excitedly. "It had to be. Did you see all that hair?"

"Yes," agreed Bogweed. "It *was* hairy, but it didn't look big enough to be a mammoth."

"It must have been a *small* mammoth then," said Fungus, jumping off the tree trunk and picking up his hunting spear.

"Come on. *We've* got dinner to catch."
Then he raced off down the path, only
slowing down long enough to make sure
Bogweed was still following him.

They went as quickly as they could,
half running and half creeping, whilst
trying not to make too much noise.

The narrow path twisted and turned as
it went deeper into the forest. A couple of
times, Fungus thought he caught sight
of a big hairy shape as it disappeared
behind a tree or turned a corner. But

each time they reached the spot where he'd seen it, they found nothing except trees and bushes.

"We've been doing this for hours," said Bogweed, when eventually they stopped for a rest. "We're probably going round in circles."

Fungus shook his head. "We can't be," he said. "Dad's taken me out hunting loads of times. I know these paths like the back of my hand."

"What path?" said Bogweed.

Fungus frowned. Bogweed was right. The path *had* disappeared. He felt a cold shiver run down his spine at the thought they might be lost, but he was determined not to let his brother know he was frightened. "Don't worry," he said. "It's got to be here somewhere."

"I hope you're right," said Bogweed. "Because it's getting dark."

"It's *always* dark in the forest," snapped Fungus.

"Yes," agreed Bogweed, looking up between the trees. "But it's getting even darker now. Just look at those clouds."

The sky above the forest was thick with black storm clouds and the first drops of rain were beginning to fall.

"We should try and find our way home," said Bogweed. "I don't want to be in the forest when this storm starts."

"Wimp!" snorted Fungus. "Don't tell me you're frightened of a bit of rain."

Bogweed opened his mouth to speak, but he was drowned out by a deafening crash as the first bolt of lightning struck. A tall tree, right next to them, exploded

26

and a huge branch fell to the floor in a shower of splinters and sparks.

"RUN!" shouted Fungus, forgetting all about being brave. He raced through the forest, with Bogweed right behind him.

Just as he had almost given up hope of finding a way out, Fungus ducked beneath an overhanging branch and found himself back on the path. "See!" he yelled. "I said I knew where I was going."

The two brothers were running at full pelt through the pouring rain. As they rounded a corner, they crashed straight into something coming in the other direction. With a heavy thud, they landed flat on their backs.

Fungus groaned and rubbed his eyes. Bogweed shook his head and stared upwards. In the shadowy darkness, all they could see was a big shape looming over them, but as a second bolt of lightning lit up the sky, they saw two incredibly hairy legs and, staring down at them, two wild-looking eyes.

Fungus and Bogweed opened their mouths and screamed at the tops of their voices, but the sound was drowned out as another clap of thunder shook the trees.

Chapter THREE

Flora Mudcrust had planned to use her big, old mammoth fur as a rug, but Bogweed had suggested it might make a good cover for the mouth of the cave. He'd been right. The thick fur was perfect for keeping out the wind and rain, but Flora was reluctant to close it now, even though it was starting to pour down.

"Where do you think they've got to?" she asked.

Lowbrow was standing outside with a spear held tightly in his hand, water dripping from his face as he peered into the gathering gloom. As the day had gone on, he had started to feel much better. Now he was worried that Fungus and Bogweed might be in danger.

"I don't know," he replied. "Chief Hawknose said he saw them going past his cave earlier, but he didn't see where they went after that."

"You don't think they've gone into the forest, do you?" said Flora.

Lowbrow shrugged. "I hope not," he replied. "But there's nothing we can do now. We'll never find them in this storm." He shivered as lightning lit up the sky and thunder rumbled around the valley.

In the forest, Fungus and Bogweed had got to their feet and were slowly backing away from the huge, hairy creature.

"BOOM! BOOM!" it bellowed, beating its chest and staring at them wide-eyed through the pouring rain.

"What is it?" asked Fungus, nervously.

"It looks like Rufus Redwood," said Bogweed, a little uncertainly.

Rufus and Ivy Redwood lived in a treehouse close to the edge of the forest. They were both very hairy and both looked very much alike.

Now Rufus Redwood was pointing at the soggy ground. "BOOM! BOOM!" he bellowed again, and stamped his feet.

"What's he on about?" asked Fungus. "And why is he staring at us like that?"

Bogweed shook his head. "I'm not sure," he said. "But I think he's trying to tell us something."

"Well, why doesn't he just *tell* us then?" said Fungus.

"Dad says that the Redwoods aren't like other people," whispered Bogweed. "They live in a treehouse and they don't speak like we do."

Rufus was becoming frantic, stamping his feet and dancing around with his fists in front of his mouth.

"Well, I think he's completely *out* of his tree," said Fungus.

"No, he's not," said Bogweed, suddenly understanding what Rufus was doing. "He's trying to tell us about the mammoths."

"MAMMOTH!" bellowed Rufus, nodding madly and showering them both with rainwater from his straggly beard.

He stomped around a couple more times then pushed past them and disappeared between the trees.

As he watched him go, Bogweed realised it had been *Rufus* they'd seen earlier, not a mammoth, after all. But there was no time to tell Fungus.

"Come on," he said. "It looks like the mammoths are coming. We have to warn the rest of the tribe."

"But mammoths come into the valley every year," said Fungus. "What's so special about this time?"

"This year they're early," said Bogweed. "No new traps have been dug, and if the herd comes charging down the valley, people's huts could get crushed."

Fungus still didn't understand what the fuss was about, but he followed Bogweed down the narrow path.

Guessing that Rufus Redwood was going back to his treehouse, it was easy

to work out which direction they should be heading, and it wasn't long before they were out of the forest.

"We should be home soon," said Bogweed, happy to see the familiar shape of Icecap Mountain in front of them. "The path to Chief Hawknose's cave is just over there."

"But we still haven't caught anything for our dinner," complained Fungus, miserably.

"That doesn't matter," said Bogweed. "Listen!"

The rain had stopped, but the sound of thunder still rumbled around the valley. In addition, Bogweed thought he could hear another rumbling noise in the distance. It was still very faint, but he was sure it was growing steadily louder.

Getting down on his hands and knees, he placed one ear to the ground and listened. He could hear it much more clearly now. This wasn't just the rumbling of thunder, either. It was the sound of hundreds of huge feet stomping towards the valley.

The mammoths really *were* coming.

"Come on!" cried Bogweed, getting to his feet. "We have to do something. We have to try to stop the mammoths." He ran off up the path towards Chief Hawknose's cave, shouting as he went.

"Help! Help! The mammoths are coming!"

Chief Hawknose appeared outside just as Bogweed arrived at his cave. "What's all the noise about?" he asked. "What's happening?"

"The mammoths are coming," Bogweed repeated.

"Nonsense," said Chief Hawknose, with a frown. "It's too early for the mammoths. They won't be here for weeks."

"But I've heard them," said Bogweed. "Listen."

As Chief Hawknose listened, there was a flash of lightning above Icecap Mountain and thunder rumbled in the air.

Chief Hawknose smiled and shook his head. "See! It's only thunder. Now go home and stop bothering me."

"No, it's not," insisted Bogweed. "We've got to warn the rest of the tribe."

Chief Hawknose's smile disappeared. "I wouldn't expect a Mudcrust to know the difference between the sound of thunder and the sound of a herd of mammoths," he said. "But *I'm* chief of this tribe and I know what's what."

"Rufus Redwood said —"

But Chief Hawknose had already gone back inside the cave.

Bogweed could hardly believe it. "Come on," he said, turning to look at his brother. "We'll go and tell Mum and Dad. They'll know what to do."

But Bogweed was all alone. Fungus had disappeared.

Chapter FOUR

At first, Fungus had been right behind his brother as he ran up Icecap Mountain, rushing to get to Chief Hawknose's cave. Then something strange had happened.

Fungus had had an idea.

Ideas were normally Bogweed's business and Fungus had always been happy with that. *He* preferred to keep it simple, bashing things with a club or poking them with a spear. But this wasn't like one of his weedy little brother's ideas. This was definitely a Fungus idea and it involved lots of

bashing and poking. This was the sort of idea Fungus could understand.

Normally, when the mammoths came into the valley during winter, all the hunters would work together. They would dig mammoth traps – huge holes in the ground, big enough for one of the great beasts to fall into. They'd cover the holes with branches and leaves to make them harder to see, then they'd wait for a mammoth to come along.

The meat from a couple of mammoths would keep everyone fed for the rest of winter, and nothing was ever wasted. The bones would be turned into tools and weapons. The fur was used to make clothing and blankets, and covers or doors for huts. And the huge tusks would be given to the bravest hunter as a reward.

But as far as Fungus could see, there was nothing brave about just digging a hole and waiting for a mammoth to fall into it. For as long as he could remember, he'd heard stories about Flatfoot, the greatest hunter the tribe had ever known. The stories went that when Flatfoot was a boy, he'd caught a mammoth all by himself, using only his hunting spear.

FLATFOOT
the
HUNTER
AS A BOY

Fungus decided that this year *he* was going to be the one getting the mammoth tusks. Bogweed had been right. It *was* up to them to stop the mammoths, but not by running to Chief Hawknose like wet wimps. This was his chance to show everyone what a great hunter he was. In years to come, people would be telling stories about *him*.

The path that led towards Chief Hawknose's cave was quite a way behind him now, and Fungus found himself running through long wet grass. The ground was littered with chunks of rock that had fallen from Icecap Mountain, and Fungus had to pick his route carefully to avoid tripping over them.

Further ahead, there was another path that led to their own cave. As he went past, Fungus glanced towards it, but he carried on running. He didn't want anyone interfering with his plan.

As he turned a corner, a strange shape loomed in front of him and Fungus skidded to a halt. At first, he thought it was a mammoth, on its own and ahead of the herd. But as he got closer, he realised it was just a lump of rock that had fallen from Icecap Mountain.

This piece of rock was huge, though, and much wider at the top than it was at the bottom. Its odd shape would make it tricky to climb, but it would also make a great lookout spot from where he could wait for the mammoths.

Fungus leant his spear against the bottom of the rock and clambered up the side as quickly as he could. From

the top he could see the small stream that ran down from the peaks of Icecap Mountain, and beyond it the grassland that widened out until it ended in a wall of solid rock. The mouth of the valley was further round the corner, hidden from view by the huge forest trees.

There was no sign of the mammoth herd though. Fungus waited for a while.

When still nothing happened, he was about to clamber back down to the ground. Then suddenly he felt something. At first, he thought a piece of the big rock had come away beneath his feet, so he tightened his grip on its surface to steady himself. Then it happened again, and Fungus realised what was going on – the whole rock was shaking.

Fungus crawled away from the edge and carefully stood up. As soon as he got to his feet, he saw them. A huge herd of mammoths was coming down the valley. It was like watching a giant wave of brown fur. Steam rose from their bodies and their feet crushed everything in their path. It was the most amazing thing Fungus had ever seen and he waved his arms in the air and whooped with joy.

Fungus watched in amazement as the herd of mammoths came round the corner and started heading towards him. From where he was standing, he had a fantastic view. The mammoths were huge, hairy creatures with long trunks and great big tusks. The ground shook beneath their feet and his rock rattled and moved with each step they took.

It wasn't until the herd got closer that Fungus started to worry. He was having to use all his strength just to stop himself from falling off the rock. Now, as the herd of monstrous mammoths thundered past him on either side, Fungus had the horrible feeling that his great plan had gone terribly wrong.

Lowbrow and Flora were waiting by the cave entrance when Bogweed arrived home. He was gasping for breath and struggling to speak.

"Mammoths early," he panted. "Fungus gone."

"Slow down," said Flora. "*Where's* Fungus gone?"

"And what's all this about mammoths?" said Lowbrow, frowning.

Bogweed explained what had happened in the forest as quickly as he could. He told them about bumping into Rufus Redwood and what Chief Hawknose had said to him.

"If old Rufus says the mammoths are coming, then the mammoths are coming," said Lowbrow. "We'll have to sort this out."

"But what about Fungus?" said Flora, anxiously.

"I think he's gone after the herd," said Bogweed. "He was determined not to come home until he'd caught something for our dinner."

"Right," said Lowbrow, turning to Flora. "You get your sister to help warn the rest of the tribe about the mammoths. Me and Bogweed will go after Fungus."

While Flora ran off to find Fauna, Bogweed and Lowbrow headed in the opposite direction, further round the mountain. The rocky path ended at the edge of a steep cliff, but from there they had a perfect view over the rest of the valley. The rumbling sound could be heard quite clearly now, and as Lowbrow looked down, he got his first sight of the herd of mammoths as they thundered along. And there, right in the middle of them, clinging to the top of a huge rock, was his eldest son, Fungus.

Chapter FIVE

There was no way Lowbrow could get down to Fungus, but Bogweed had an idea.

"It's a good job I thought to bring my rope," he said. "And this sabre-tooth tiger's jawbone will be useful, too."

While Bogweed unravelled his rope, Mere and Chief Hawknose came running up the path.

"What's going on?" demanded Chief Hawknose. "Flora says the mammoths are here and you might need our help."

"They *are* here," said Lowbrow.

"And Fungus is trapped in the middle of the herd."

Chief Hawknose peered over the edge of the cliff, and could hardly believe his eyes. "But they shouldn't be here for weeks," he spluttered. "They're early."

"Yes!" agreed Lowbrow. "And you're late, so keep out of the way."

"What are you going to do?" asked Mere.

"We're going to rescue him," said Bogweed, as he fastened one end of his vine rope to Lowbrow's biggest hunting spear. "Now, Dad, do you think you could throw your spear into those trees?"

Lowbrow looked over the edge of the cliff at the trees Bogweed was pointing to, and frowned. It was a long way.

"All the way to the forest," snorted

Chief Hawknose. "No one can throw a spear that far."

"Oh no!" said Lowbrow, scowling. "Just you watch."

He picked up the big hunting spear and ran. Just before he got to the edge of the cliff, Lowbrow stopped and hurled the weapon with all his might.

The heavy spear flew through the air, dragging Bogweed's vine rope behind it.

"I hope the rope's long enough," said

Bogweed, as the spear shot high over Fungus's head and disappeared into the trees far below.

Chief Hawknose stared in amazement. "That's –"

"Humph," huffed Lowbrow. "Not as far as I wanted."

"That's perfect," said Bogweed, tugging on the rope to make sure the spear was lodged firmly in the trees. "Now, can you tie this end around a big rock?"

Lowbrow pulled the rope as tightly as he could and Mere tied it around a rock while Bogweed made sure it was in the right position. When they'd finished, the rope stretched out over the valley, above Fungus's head and into the forest.

"There," said Lowbrow. "Now what?"

"Now it's my turn," Bogweed grinned.

And, before anyone could say anything, Bogweed had hooked the sabre-tooth tiger's jawbone over the rope and jumped off the side of the mountain.

Fungus was terrified. The rock he was holding onto was shaking furiously as the mammoths charged past. He was close enough to hear their snorting breath and smell the stench of their wet fur. Some of them waved their great trunks in the air and shook their terrible tusks. Every now and then, one of the huge beasts would brush against his rock, making it wobble even more. The whole thing could topple over at any minute, throwing him at the feet of the herd.

Fungus was wishing he'd gone home with Bogweed instead of wanting to be a brave hunter like Flatfoot. If he fell off the rock, it would be more than just his foot that would be squashed.

At that moment, Fungus happened to glance up, and he was just in time to see his

brother leaping from the edge of Icecap Mountain. But instead of falling straight down, Bogweed came whizzing towards him along a rope.

Fungus didn't know what Bogweed was up to, but he knew a way out when he saw one.

As his brother flew overhead, Fungus reached up and grabbed hold of his legs. He felt himself being lifted from the top of the rock just as the whole thing toppled over. There was a terrible racket from the herd below, but Fungus was too busy holding on tight to look down.

A minute later, they landed in the trees with a splintering crunch, shaken and bruised, but luckily not seriously hurt.

"You clumsy wimp," yelled Fungus. "You've landed on my head!"

"You stinking hog," complained Bogweed. "You're standing on my hand!"

As they untangled themselves from

the branches of the tree, the brothers grinned at each other.

"Thanks," said Fungus. "That was pretty cool."

"Yes," agreed Bogweed. "It was."

By the time Bogweed and Fungus had clambered out of the tree, most of the mammoth herd had passed. They watched in silence as the last few stragglers thundered by.

The long grass between the forest and the mountain had been squashed flat and there were deep footprints everywhere. A group of people had gathered round the big rock and more were coming along the valley. The two brothers rushed towards the crowd of people. Among them, they saw their parents with Mere and Fauna.

Chief Hawknose was following close behind.

"The tribe's all right," shouted Mere, running to join Bogweed and Fungus.

"Yes," agreed Fauna. "Thanks to Bogweed, we managed to warn everyone just in time."

"Some of the huts were flattened though," said Mere. "People have lost their homes."

"But what about you two?" asked Flora, looking worriedly at her sons.

"We're fine," said Fungus.

"Just a couple of scratches," said Bogweed.

Chief Hawknose, looking very red in the face, smiled weakly. "We were all very lucky," he said.

Lowbrow smiled proudly at his sons. "It looks like the mammoths are now safely out of the way at the end of the valley." He turned to Chief Hawknose. "But these people are going to need somewhere to stay until we can rebuild their huts."

"I know that," snapped Chief Hawknose. "I *am* the chief of this tribe."

"Well, then it's *your* job to find them somewhere to live," said Lowbrow.

"But there's nowhere for them to go," said Chief Hawknose. "There are no more caves."

"Then they'll have to stay with *you*," said Lowbrow.

"But that's impossible," spluttered Chief Hawknose. "We haven't got enough room."

"I'm sure you'll manage," said Lowbrow with a smile. "But at least there's *some* good news. It looks like someone's killed a mammoth!"

Bogweed and Fungus looked puzzled for a moment, but as they made their way through the crowd of people, sure enough, they saw the mammoth. The big rock Fungus had been standing on had fallen over, crushing the creature beneath it.

"Ha!" shouted Chief Hawknose. "This mammoth was killed by the rock. Not by a hunter. That means the tusks go to the chief. That *is* good news."

"Wait just one minute," said Lowbrow, crouching down. "What's this?" He pulled out something from beneath the great beast's dead body. It was a hunting spear, broken and covered in blood.

"Who does this spear belong to?" shouted Lowbrow, holding it in the air for all to see.

Everyone looked at the hunting spear in silence. Fungus's jaw dropped open and he raised his hand. "It's mine," he said.

A huge cheer went up from the crowd and Fungus grinned from ear to ear as people rushed forward to congratulate him.

FUNGUS the HERO!

"Listen!" cried Chief Hawknose. "This is nonsense. Everyone knows Fungus couldn't have killed a mammoth on his own."

For once, no one paid any attention to what their chief was saying. Instead, they lifted Fungus up onto their shoulders and carried him off, cheering.

"You've had your chance to make people listen to you," said Lowbrow. "You could have warned them about the mammoth herd. But you didn't believe what my son told you."

"But they *have* to listen to me," insisted Hawknose. "I'm their chief."

"Things are changing round here," said Lowbrow. "And I think it's time we had a *new* chief."

Chief Hawknose opened his mouth

to speak, but closed it again and glared at Lowbrow before storming back towards his cave. If Lowbrow Mudcrust thought he was good enough to become chief, then so be it. He'd beaten him once in the chief trials and he'd beat him again. He had plenty of tricks up his fur sleeve to make sure about that.

Flora Mudcrust smiled proudly to herself as they walked home. There would be mammoth steak for dinner tonight, her sons were heroes, and soon her husband might become chief of the tribe. Even the coming winter couldn't spoil things now.